CONCERNING
THE ECCENTRICITIES OF
CARDINAL PIRELLI

RONALD FIRBANK

DUCKWORTH

This impression 1977

First published in England 1926

Gerald Duckworth & Co. Ltd.
The Old Piano Factory
43 Gloucester Crescent, London NW1

ISBN 0 7156 1095 3 (cased)
ISBN 0 7156 1099 6 (paper)

Printed in Great Britain
by Unwin Brothers Limited,
The Gresham Press, Old Woking, Surrey

HUDDLED up in a cope of gold wrought silk he peered around. Society had rallied in force. A christening— and not a child's.

Rarely had he witnessed, before the font, so many brilliant people. Were it an heir to the DunEden acres (instead of what it *was*) the ceremony could have hardly drawn together a more distinguished throng.

Monsignor Silex moved a finger from forehead to chin, and from ear to ear. The Duquesa DunEden's escapades, if continued, would certainly cost the Cardinal his hat.

"And ease my heart by splashing fountains."

From the choir-loft a boy's young voice was evoking Heaven.

"His hat!" Monsignor Silex exclaimed aloud, blinking a little at the immemorial font of black Macæl marble that had provoked the screams of pale number-less babies.

Here Saints and Kings had been baptized, and royal Infantas, and sweet Poets, whose high names thrilled the heart.

Monsignor Silex crossed his breast. He must gather force to look about him. Frame a close report. The Pontiff, in far-off Italy, would expect precision.

Beneath the state baldequin, or Grand Xaymaca, his Eminence sat enthroned ogled by the wives of a dozen grandees. The Altamissals, the Villarasas (their grandee-ships' approving glances, indeed, almost eclipsed their wives'), and Catherine, Countess of Constantine, the most talked-of beauty in the realm, looking like some wild limb of Astaroth in a little crushed " toreador " hat round as an athlete's coif with hanging silken balls, while beside her a stout, dumpish dame, of enormous persuasion, was joggling, solicitously, an object that was of the liveliest interest to all.

Head archly bent, her fine arms divined through darkling laces, the Duquesa stood, clasping closely a week-old police-dog in the ripple of her gown.

" Mother's pet! " she cooed, as the imperious creature passed his tongue across the splendid uncertainty of her chin.

Monsignor Silex's large, livid face grew grim.

What,—disquieting doubt,—if it were her Grace's offspring after all? Praise heaven, he was ignorant enough regarding the schemes of nature, but in an old lutrin once he had read of a young woman engendering a missel-thrush through the channel of her nose. It had created a good deal of scandal to be sure at the time: the Holy Inquisition, indeed, had condemned the impudent baggage, in consequence, to the stake.

" That was the style to treat them," he murmured, appraising the assembly with no kindly eye. The presence of Madame San Seymour surprised him; one habitually so set apart and devout! And Madame La Urench, too, gurgling away freely to the four-legged Father: " No, my naughty Blessing; no, not now! . . . By and by, a *bone*."

Words which brought the warm saliva to the expectant parent's mouth.

Tail awag, sex apparent (to the affected slight confusion of the Infanta Eulalia-Irene), he crouched, his eyes fixed wistfully upon the nozzle of his son.

Ah, happy delirium of first parenthood! Adoring pride! Since times primæval by what masonry does it knit together those that have succeeded in establishing here, on earth, the vital bonds of a family's claim?

Even the modest sacristan, at attention by the font, felt himself to be superior of parts to a certain unproductive chieftain of a princely House, who had lately undergone a course of asses' milk in the surrounding mountains—all in vain!

But, supported by the Prior of the Cartuja, the Cardinal had arisen for the act of Immersion.

Of unusual elegance, and with the remains, moreover, of perfect looks, he was as wooed and run after by the ladies as any *matador*.

" And thus being cleansed and purified, I do call thee ' Crack '! " he addressed the Duquesa's captive burden.

Tail sheathed with legs " in master's drawers," ears cocked, tongue pendent. . . .

"Mother's mascot! "

" Oh, take care, dear; he's removing all your rouge! "

" *What?* "

" He's spoilt, I fear, your roses." The Countess of Constantine tittered.

The Duquesa's grasp relaxed. To be seen by all the world at this disadvantage.

" Both? " she asked, distressed, disregarding the culprit, who sprang from her breast with a sharp, sportive bark.

What rapture, what freedom!

" Misericordia! " Monsignor Silex exclaimed, staring aghast at a leg poised, inconsequently, against the mural-tablet of the widowed duchess of Charona—a woman who, in her lifetime, had given over thirty million pezos to the poor!

Ave Maria purissima! What challenging snarls and measured mystery marked the elaborate recognition of father and son, and would no one then forbid their incestuous frolics?

In agitation Monsignor Silex sought fortitude from

3

the storied windows overhead, aglow in the ambered light as some radiant missal.

It was. Saint Eufraxia's Eve, she of Egypt, a frail unit numbered above among the train of the Eleven Thousand Virgins: an immaturish schoolgirl of a saint, unskilled, inexperienced in handling a prayer, lacking the vim and native astuteness of the incomparable Theresa.

Yes; divine interference, 'twixt father and son, was hardly to be looked for, and Eufraxia (she of Egypt) had failed too often before. . . .

Monsignor Silex started slightly, as, from the estrade beneath the dome, a choir-boy let fall a little white spit.

Dear child, as though *that* would part them!

" Things must be allowed to take their ' natural ' course," he concluded, following the esoteric antics of the reunited pair.

Out into the open, over the Lapis Lazuli of the floor, they flashed, with stifled yelps, like things possessed.

" He'll tear my husband's drawers! " the duquesa lamented.

" The duque's legs. Poor Decima." The Infanta fell quietly to her knees.

" Fortify . . . asses . . . " the royal lips moved.

" Brave darling," she murmured, gently rising.

But the duquesa had withdrawn, it seemed, to repair her ravaged roses, and from the obscurity of an adjacent confessional-box was calling to order Crack.

" Come, Crack! "

And to the Mauro-Hispanic rafters the echo rose.

" Crack, Crack, Crack, Crack. . . ."

I I

FROM the Calle de la Pasión, beneath the blue-tiled mirador of the garden wall, came the soft brooding sound of a seguidilla. It was a twilight planned for wooing, unbending, consent; many, before now, had come to grief on an evening such. " It was the moon."

Pacing a cloistered walk, laden with the odour of sun-tired flowers, the Cardinal could not but feel the insidious influences astir. The bells of the institutions of the *Encarnacion* and the Immaculate Conception, joined in confirming Angelus, had put on tones half-bridal, enough to create vague longings, or sudden tears, among the young patrician boarders.

" Their parents' daughters—convent-bred," the Cardinal sighed.

At the Immaculate Conception, dubbed by, the Queen, in irony, once " The school for harlots," the little Infanta Maria-Paz must be lusting for her Mamma and the Court, and the lilac carnage of the ring, while chafing also in the same loose captivity would be the roguish *niñas* of the pleasure-loving duchess of Sarmento, girls whose Hellenic ethics had given the good Abbess more than one attack of fullness.

Morality. Poise! For without temperance and equilibrium—— The Cardinal halted.

But in the shifting underlight about him the flushed camellias and the sweet night-jasmines suggested none; neither did the shape of a garden-Eros pointing radiantly the dusk.

" For unless we have balance——" the Cardinal murmured, distraught, admiring against the elusive nuances of the afterglow the cupid's voluptuous hams.

5

It was against these, once, in a tempestuous mood that his mistress had smashed her fan-sticks.

"Would that all liaisons would break as easily!" his Eminence framed the prayer: and musing on the appalling constancy of a certain type, he sauntered leisurely on. Yes, enveloping women like Luna Sainz, with their lachrymose, tactless "mys," how shake them off? "My" Saviour, "my" lover, "my" parasol—and, even, "my" virtue. . . .

"Poor dearie."

The Cardinal smiled.

Yet once in a way, perhaps, he was not averse to being favoured by a glimpse of her: "A little visit on a night like this." Don Alvaro Narciso Hernando Pirelli, Cardinal-Archbishop of Clemenza, smiled again.

In the gloom there, among the high thickets of bay and flowering myrtle. . . . For, after all, bless her, one could not well deny she possessed the chief essentials: "such, poor soul, as they are!" he reflected, turning about at the sound as of the neigh of a horse.

"Monseigneur. . . ."

Bearing a biretta and a silver shawl, Madame Poco, the venerable Superintendent-of-the-palace, looking, in the blue moonlight, like some whiskered skull, emerged, after inconceivable peepings, from among the leafy limbo of the trees.

"Ah, Don Alvaro, sir! Come here."

"Pest!" His Eminence evinced a touch of asperity.

"Ah, Don, Don, . . ." and skimming forward with the grace of a Torero lassooing a bull, she slipped the scintillating fabric about the prelate's neck.

"Such nights breed fever, Don Alvaro, and there is mischief in the air."

"Mischief?"

"In certain quarters of the city you would take it almost for some sortilege."

6

" What next? "

" At the *Encarnacion* there's nothing, of late, but seediness. Sister Engracia with the chicken-pox, and Mother Claridad with the itch, while at the College of Noble Damosels, in the Calle Santa Fé, I hear a daughter of Don José Illescas, in a fit of caprice, has set a match to her coronet."

" A match to her what? "

" And how explain, Don Alvaro of my heart, these constant shots in the Cortès? Ah, *sangre mio*, in what times we live! "

Ambling a few steps pensively side by side, they moved through the brilliant moonlight. It was the hour when the awakening fireflies are first seen like atoms of rosy flame floating from flower to flower.

" Singular times, sure enough," the Cardinal answered, pausing to enjoy the transparent beauty of the white dripping water of a flowing fountain.

" And ease my heart by splashing—tum-tiddly-um-tum," he hummed. "I trust the choir-boys, Dame, are all in health? "

" Ah, Don Alvaro, no, sir! "

" Eh? "

" No, sir," Madame Poco murmured, taking up a thousand golden poses.

" Why, how's that? "

" But few now seem keen on Leapfrog, or Bossage, and when a boy shows no wish for a game of Leap, sir, or Bossage——"

" Exactly," his Eminence nodded.

" I'm told it's some time, young cubs, since they've played pranks on Tourists! Though only this afternoon little Ramón Ragatta came over queazy while demonstrating before foreigners the Dance of the Arc, which should teach him in future not to be so profane: and as to the acolytes, Don Alvaro, at least half

7

of them are absent, confined to their cots, in the wards of the pistache Fathers!"

"To-morrow, all well, I'll take them some melons."

"Ah, Don, Don!!"

"And, perhaps, a cucumber," the Cardinal added, turning valedictionally away.

The tones of the seguidilla had deepened and from the remote recesses of the garden arose a bedlam of nightingales and frogs.

It was certainly incredible how he felt immured.

Yet to forsake the Palace for the Plaza he was obliged to stoop to creep.

With the Pirelli pride, with resourceful intimacy he communed with his heart: deception is a humiliation; but humiliation is a Virtue—a Cardinal, like myself, and one of the delicate violets of our Lady's crown. . . . Incontestably, too,—he had a flash of inconsequent insight, many a prod to a discourse, many a sapient thrust, delivered ex cathedrâ, amid the broken sobs of either sex, had been inspired, before now, by what prurient persons might term, perhaps, a "frolic." But away with all scruples! Once in the street in mufti, how foolish they became.

The dear street. The adorable Avenidas. The quickening stimulus of the crowd: truly it was exhilarating to mingle freely with the throng!

Disguised as a cabellero from the provinces or as a matron (disliking to forgo altogether the militant bravoura of a skirt), it became possible to combine philosophy, equally, with pleasure.

The promenade at the Trinidades seldom failed to be diverting, especially when the brown Bettita or the Ortiz danced! *Olé*, he swayed his shawl. The Argentina with Blanca Sanchez was amusing too; her ear-tickling little song "Madrid is on the Manzan-

ares," trailing the " 'ares " indefinitely, was sure, in
due course, to reach the Cloisters.

Deliberating critically on the numerous actresses
of his diocese, he traversed lightly a path all enclosed
by pots of bergamot.

And how entrancing to perch on a bar-stool, over
a glass of old golden sherry!

" Ah Jesus-Maria," he addressed the dancing lightning in the sky.

Purring to himself, and frequently pausing, he
made his way, by ecstatic degrees, towards the mirador
on the garden wall.

Although a mortification, it was imperative to bear
in mind the consequences of cutting a too dashing
figure. Beware display. Vanity once had proved all
but fatal: " I remember it was the night I wore ringlets
and was called ' my queen.' "

And with a fleeting smile, Don Alvaro Pirelli recalled the persistent officer who had had the effrontery
to attempt to molest him: " Stalked me the whole
length of the Avenue Isadora! " It had been a lesson.
" Better to be on the drab side," he reflected, turning
the key of the garden tower.

Dating from the period of the Reformation of the
Nunneries, it commanded the privacy of many a
drowsy patio.

" I see the Infanta has begun her Tuesdays! " he
serenely noted, sweeping the panorama with a glance.

It was a delightful prospect.

Like some great guitar the city lay engirdled ethe-
really by the snowy Sierras.

" Foolish featherhead," he murmured, his glance
falling upon a sunshade of sapphire chiffon, left by
Luna: " ' my ' parasol! " he twirled the crystal
hilt.

" Everything she forgets, bless her," he breathed,
lifting his gaze towards the magnolia blossom cups

that overtopped the tower, stained by the eternal treachery of the night to the azure of the Saint Virgin: Suspended in the miracle of the moonlight their elfin globes were at their zenith.

" Madrid is on the Manzan-ares," he intoned.

But " Clemenza," of course, is in white Andalucia.

III

AFTER the tobacco-factory and the railway-station, quite the liveliest spot in all the city was the cathedral-sacristia. In the interim of an Office it would be besieged by the laity, often to the point of scrimmage: aristocrats and mendicants, relatives of acolytes—each had some truck or other in the long lofty room. Here the secretary of the chapter, a burly little man, a sound judge of women and bulls, might be consulted gratis, preferably before the supreme heat of day. Seated beneath a sombre study of the Magdalen waylaying our Lord (a work of wistful interest ascribed to Valdés Leal), he was, with tactful courtesy, at the disposal of anyone soliciting information as to " vacant dates," or " hours available," for some impromptu function. Indulgences, novenas, terms for special masses—with flowers and music? Or, just plain; the expense, it varied! Bookings for baptisms, it was certainly advisable to book well ahead; some mothers booked before the birth—; ah-hah, the little Juans and Juanas; the angelic babies! And arrangements for a corpse's lying-in-state: " Leave it to me." These, and such things, were in his province.

But the secretarial bureau was but merely a speck in the vast shuttered room. As a rule, it was by the old pagan sarcophaguses, outside the vestry-door, " waiting for Father," that *aficianados* of the cult liked best to foregather.

It was the morning of the Feast of San Antolin of Panticosa, a morning so sweet, and blue and luminous, and many were waiting.

" It's queer the time a man takes to slip on a frilly!"

the laundress of the Basilica, Doña Consolacion, observed, through her fansticks, to Tomás the beadle.

" Got up as you get them. . . ."

" It's true, indeed, I've a knack with a rochet! "

" Temperament will out, Doña Consolacion; it cannot be hid."

The laundress beamed.

" Mine's the French."

" It's God will *whatever* it is."

" It's the French," she lisped, considering the silver rings on her honey-brown hands. Of distinguished presence, with dark matted curls at either ear, she was the apotheosis of flesh triumphant.

But the entry from the vestry of a file of monsignore imposed a transient silence—a silence which was broken only by the murmur of passing mule bells along the street.

Tingaling, tingaling: evocative of grain and harvest the sylvan sound of mule bells came and went.

Doña Consolacion flapped her fan.

There was to be question directly of a Maiden Mass.

With his family all about him, the celebrant, a youth of the People, looking childishly happy in his first broidered cope, had bent, more than once, his good-natured head, to allow some small brothers and sisters to inspect his tonsure.

" Like a little, little star! "

" No. Like a *perra gorda*."

" No, like a little star," they fluted, while an irrepressible grandmother, moved to tears and laughter, insisted on planting a kiss on the old " Christian " symbol. " He'll be a Pope some day, if he's spared! " she sobbed, transported.

" Not he, the big burly bull." Mother Garcia of the Company of Jesus addressed Doña Consolacion with a mellifluent chuckle.

Holding a bouquet of sunflowers and a basket of eggs she had just looked in from Market.

" Who knows, my dear? " Doña Consolacion returned, fixing her gaze upon an Epitaph on a vault beneath her feet. " ' He was a boy and she dazzled him.' Heigh-ho! Heysey-ho . . .! Yes, as I was saying."

" Pho: I'd like to see him in a Papal tiara."

" It's mostly luck. I well recall his Eminence when he was nothing but a trumpery curate," Doña Consolacion declared, turning to admire the jewelled studs in the ears of the President of the College of Noble Damosels.

" Faugh! " Mother Garcia spat.

" It's all luck."

" There's luck and luck," the beadle put in. Once he had confined by accident a lady in the souterrains of the cathedral, and only many days later had her bones and a diary, a diary documenting the most delicate phases of solitude and loneliness, *a woman's contribution to Science*, come to light; a piece of carelessness that had gone against the old man in his preferment.

" Some careers are less fortunate than others," Mother Garcia exclaimed, appraising the sleek silhouette of Monsignor Silex, then precipitantly issuing from the Muniment-Room.

It was known he was not averse to a little stimulant in the bright middle of the morning.

" He has the evil Eye, dear, he has the evil Eye," Doña Consolacion murmured, averting her head. Above her hung a sombre Ribera, in a frame of elaborate, blackened gilding.

" Ah, well, I do not fear it," the Companion of Jesus answered, making way for a dark, heavy belle in a handkerchief and shawl.

" Has anyone seen Jositto, my little José? "

Mother Garcia waved with her bouquet towards an adjacent portal, surmounted, with cool sobriety,

by a long, lavender marble cross. " I expect he's
through there."

" In the cathedral? "

" How pretty you look, dear, and what a very gay
shawl! "

" Pure silk."

" I don't *doubt* it! "

Few women, however, are indifferent to the seduc-
tion of a Maiden Mass, and all in a second there was
scarcely one to be found in the whole sacristia.

The secretary at his bureau looked about him:
without the presence of *las mujares* the atmosphere
seemed to weigh a little; still, being a Holiday of
Obligation, a fair sprinkling of boys, youthful chapter
hands whom he would sometimes designate as the
" lesser delights," relieved the place of its austerity.

Through the heraldic windows, swathed in straw-
mats to shut out the heat, the sun-rays entered, tattoo-
ing with piquant freckles the pampered faces of the
choir.

A request for a permit to view the fabled Orangery
in the cloisters interrupted his siestose fancies.

Like luxurious cygnets in their cloudy lawn, a score
of young singing-boys were awaiting their cue: Low-
masses, cheapness, and economy, how they despised
them, and how they would laugh at " Old Ends "
who snuffed out the candles.

" Why should the Church charge *higher* for a short
Magnificat than for a long *Miserere?* "

The question had just been put by the owner of a
dawning moustache and a snub, though expressive,
nose.

" Because happiness makes people generous, stupid,
and often as not they'll squander, boom, but un-
happiness makes them calculate. People grudge spend-
ing much on a snivel—even if it lasts an hour."

" It's the choir that suffers."

"This profiteering . . . The Chapter . . ." there was a confusion of voices.

"Order!" A slim lad, of an ambered paleness, raised a protesting hand. Indulged, and made-much-of by the hierarchy, he was Felix Ganay, known as Chief-dancing-choir-boy to the cathedral of Clemenza.

"Aren't they awful?" he addressed a child with a very finished small head. Fingering a score of music he had been taking lead in a mass of Palestrina, and had the vaguely distraught air of a kitten that had seen visions.

"After that, I've not a dry stitch on me," he murmured, with a glance towards the secretary, who was making lost grimaces at the Magdalen's portrait.

A lively controversy (becoming increasingly more shrill) was dividing the acolytes and choir.

"Tiny and Tibi! Enough." The intervention came from the full-voiced Christobal, a youngster of fifteen, with soft, peach-textured cheeks, and a tongue never far away. Considered an opportunist, he was one of the privileged six dancing-boys of the cathedral.

"Order!" Felix enjoined anew. Finely sensitive as to his prerogatives, the interference of his colleague was apt to vex him. He would be trying to clip an altar pose next. Indeed, it was a matter of scandal already, how he was attempting to attract attention, in influential places, by the unnecessary undulation of his loins, and by affecting strong scents and attars, such as Egyptian Tahetant, or Long flirt through the violet Hours. Himself, Felix, he was faithful to Royal Florida, or even to plain *eau-de-Cologne*, and to those slow Mozarabic movements which alone are seemly to the Church.

"You may mind your business, young Christobal," Felix murmured, turning towards a big, serious, melancholy boy, who was describing a cigarette-case he had received as fee for singing "Say it with Edelweiss" at a society wedding.

" Say it with what? " the cry came from an on-coming-looking child, with caressing liquid eyes, and a little tongue the colour of raspberry-cream—*so bright*. Friend of all sweets and dainties, he held San Antolin's day chiefly notable for the Saint's sweet biscuits, made of sugar and white-of-egg.

" And you, too, Chicklet. Mind your business, can't you? " Felix exclaimed, appraising in some dismay a big, bland woman, then descending upon the secretary at his desk, with a slow, but determined, waddle.

Amalia Bermudez, the fashionable Actress-manageress of the Teatro Victoria Eugenia, was becoming a source of terror to the chapter of Clemenza. Every morning, with fatal persistence, she would aboard the half-hypnotised secretary with the request that the Church should make " a little christian " of her blue chow, for unless it could be done it seemed the poor thing wasn't *chic*. To be *chic* and among the foremost vanward; this, apart from the Theatre, meant all to her in life, and since the unorthodox affair of " the DunEdens," she had been quite upset by the chapter's evasive refusals.

" If a police-dog, then why not a chow? " she would ask. " Why not my little Whisky? Little devil. Ah, believe me, Father, she has need of it; for she's supposed to have had a snake by my old dog Conqueror! . . . And yet you won't receive her? Oh, it's heartless. Men are cruel. . . ."

" There she is! Amalia—the Bermudez ": the whisper spread, arresting the story of the black Bishop of Bechuanaland, just begun by the roguish Ramón.

And in the passing silence the treble voice of Tiny was left talking all alone.

" . . . frightened me like Father did, when he kissed me in the dark like a lion ":—a remark that was greeted by an explosion of coughs.

16

But this morning the clear, light laugh of the comedienne rang out merrily. "No, no, *hombre,*" she exclaimed (tapping the secretary upon the cheek archly with her fan), "now don't, don't stare at me, and intimidate me like that! I desire only to offer ' a Mass of Intention,' fully choral, *that the Church may change her mind.*"

And when the cannon that told of Noon was fired from the white fortress by the river far away she was still considering programmes of music by Rossini and Cimarosa, and the colour of the chasubles which the clergy should wear.

IV

AT the season when the oleanders are in their full perfection, their choicest bloom, it was the Pontiff's innovation to install his American type-writing apparatus in the long Loggie of the Apostolic Palace that had been in disuse since the demise of Innocent XVI. Out-of-doorish, as Neapolitans usually are, Pope Tertius II was no exception to the rule, preferring blue skies to golden ceilings—a taste for which indeed many were inclined to blame him. A compromise between the state-saloons and the modest suite occupied by his Holiness from choice, these open Loggie, adorned with the radiant frescoes of Luca Signorelli, would be frequently the scene of some particular Audience, granted after the exacting press of official routine.

Late one afternoon the Pontiff after an eventful and arduous day was walking thoughtfully here alone. Participating no longer in the joys of the world, it was, however, charming to catch, from time to time, the distant sound of Rome—the fitful clamour of trams and cabs, and the plash of the great twin-fountains in the court of Saint Damascus.

Wrapped in grave absorption, with level gaze, the lips slightly pinched, Pope Tertius II paced to and fro, occasionally raising a well-formed (though hairy) hand, as though to dismiss his thoughts with a benediction. The nomination of two Vacant Hats, the marriage annulment of an ex-hereditary Grand Duchess, and the " scandals of Clemenza," were equally claiming his attention and ruffling his serenity.

He had the head of an elderly lady's-maid, and an expression concealed by layers of tactful caution.

" Why can't they all behave? " he asked himself plaintively, descrying Lucrezia, his prized white squirrel, sidling shyly towards him.

She was the gift of the Archbishop of Trebizond, who had found her in the region of the Coelian hill.

" Slyboots, slyboots," Pope Tertius exclaimed, as she skipped from reach. It was incredible with what playful zest she would spring from statue to statue; and it would have amused the Vicar of Christ to watch her slip and slide, had it not suggested many a profound moral metaphor applicable to the Church. " Gently, gently," he enjoined; for once, in her struggles, she had robbed a fig-leaf off a " Moses."

" Yes, why can't they all behave? " he murmured, gazing up into the far pale-blueness.

He stood a brief moment transfixed, as if in prayer, oblivious of two whispering chamberlains.

It was the turn-in-waiting of Baron Oschatz, a man of engaging exquisite manners, and of Count Cuenca, an individual who seemed to be in perpetual consternation.

Depositing a few of the most recent camera portraits of the Pontiff requiring autograph in a spot where he could not fail but see them, they formally withdrew.

It had been a day distinguished by innumerable Audiences, several not uninteresting to recall. . . .

Certainly the increasing numbers of English were decidedly promising, and bore out the sibylline predictions of their late great and sagacious ruler—Queen Victoria.

" The dear *santissima* woman," the Pontiff sighed, for he entertained a sincere, if brackish, enthusiasm for the lady who for so many years had corresponded with the Holy See under the signature of *the Countess of Lostwaters*.

" Anglicans . . . ? Heliolatries and sun-worshippers," she had written in her most masterful hand, " and your Holiness may believe us," she had added, " when we say especially our beloved Scotch."

" I shouldn't wonder enormously if it were true," the Pope exclaimed, catching through a half-shut door a glimpse of violet stockings.

Such a display of old, out-at-heel hose could but belong to Cardinal Robin.

There had been a meeting of the Board for Extraordinary Ecclesiastical Affairs, and when, shortly afterwards, the Cardinal was admitted he bore still about him some remote trace of faction.

He had the air of a cuttle-fish, and an inquiring voice. Inclined to gesture, how many miles must his hands have moved in the course of the sermons that he had preached!

Saluting the sovereign Pontiff with a deep obeisance, the Cardinal came directly to the point.

" These schisms in Spain . . ."

" They are ever before me," His Holiness confessed.

" With priests like Pirelli, the Church is in peril! " the Cardinal declared, with a short, abysmal laugh.

" Does he suppose we are in the times of Baal and Moloch? " the Pope asked, pressing a harassed hand to his head. A Neapolitan of Naples (O Bay of Napoli. See Vesuvius, *and die*), he had curly hair that seemed to grow visibly; every few hours his tonsure would threaten to disappear.

The Cardinal sent up his brows a little.

" If I may tender the advice of the secret Consistory," he said, " your Holiness should Listen-in."

" To what end? "

" A snarl, a growl, a bark, a yelp, coming from the font, would be quite enough to condemn . . ."

"Per Bacco. I should take it for a baby."

" . . . condemn," the Cardinal pursued, " this Pirelli for a *maleficus pastor*. In which case, the earlier, the better, the unfrocking. . . ."

The Pontiff sighed.

The excellent Cardinal was as fatiguing as a mission from Salt Lake City.

" Evidently," he murmured, detecting traces of rats among the papyrus plants in the long walk below.

" They come up from the Tiber! " he exclaimed, piloting the Cardinal dexterously towards a flight of footworn steps leading to the Court of Bramante.

" It's a bore there being no lift! " he commented (the remark was a Vatican cliché), dismissing the Cardinal with a benediction.

" A painful interview," the Holy Father reflected, regarding the Western sky. An evening rose and radiant altogether. . . .

Turning sadly, he perceived Count Cuenca.

A nephew of the Dean of the Sacred College, it was rumoured that he was addicted, in his " home " above Frascati, to the last excesses of the pre-Adamite Sultans.

" A dozen blessings, for a dozen Hymens—but only eleven were sent," he was babbling distractedly to himself. He had been unstrung all day, " just a mass of foolish nerves," owing to a woman, an American, it seemed, coming for her Audience in a hat edged with white and yellow water-lilies. She had been repulsed successfully by the Papal Guard, but it had left an unpleasant impression.

" How's that? " the Vicar of Christ exclaimed: he enjoyed to tease his Chamberlains—especially Count Cuenca.

The Count turned pale.

" ——," he replied inaudibly, rolling eyes at Lucrezia.

Baron Oschatz had " deserted" him; and what is one Chamberlain, alas, without another?

" The photographs of your Holiness are beside the

bust of Bernini!" he stammered out, beating a diplomatic retreat.

Pope Tertius II addressed his squirrel.

"Little slyboots," he said, "I often laugh when I'm alone."

V

BEFORE the white façade of the DunEden Palace,
commanding the long, palm-shaded Paseo del Violôn,
an array of carriages and limousines was waiting;
while, passing in brisk succession beneath the portico,
like a swarm of brilliant butterflies, each instant was
bringing more. Dating from the period of Don Pedro
el cruel, the palace had been once the residence of the
famous Princesse des Ursins, who had left behind
something of her conviviality and glamour. But it is
unlikely that the soirées of the exuberant and fanciful
Princesse eclipsed those of the no less exuberant
Duquesa DunEden. It was to be an evening (flavoured
with rich heroics) in honour of the convalescence of
several great ladies, from an attack of " Boheara," the
new and fashionable epidemic, diagnosed by the
medical faculty as " hyperæsthesia with complica-
tions "; a welcoming back to the world in fact of
several despotic dowagers, not one perhaps of whom,
had she departed this life, would have been really
much missed or mourned! And thus, in deference to
the intimate nature of the occasion, it was felt by the
solicitous hostess that a Tertulia (that mutual exchange
of familiar or intellectual ideas) would make less
demand on arms and legs than would a ball: just the
mind and lips . . . a skilful rounding-off here, de-
veloping there, chiselling, and putting-out feelers;
an evening dedicated to the furtherance of intrigue,
scandal, love, beneath the eager eyes of a few young
girls, still at school, to whom a quiet party was per-
mitted now and then.

Fingering a knotted scapular beneath a windy arch

Mother Saint-Mary-of-the-Angels was asking God His will. Should she wait for Gloria and Clyte (they might be some time) or return to the convent and come back again at twelve? " The dear girls are with their mother," she informed her Maker, inclining respectfully before the Princess Aurora of the Asturias, who had just arrived attended by two bearded gentlemen with tummies.

Hopeful of glimpsing perhaps a colleague, Mother Saint-Mary moved a few steps impulsively in their wake. It was known that Monseigneur the Cardinal-Archbishop himself was expected, and not infrequently one ecclesiastic will beget another.

The crimson saloon, with its scattered group of chairs, was waxing cheery.

Being the day it was, and the social round never but slightly varying, most of the guests had flocked earlier in the evening to the self-same place, i.e. the Circus, or *Arena Amanda*, where it was subscription night, and where, at present, there was an irresistibly comic clown.

" One has only to think of him to——! " the wife of the Minister of Public Instruction exclaimed, going off into a fit of wheezy laughter.

" What power, what genius, what——! " The young wife of the Inspector of Rivers and Forests was at a loss. Wedded to one of the handsomest though dullest of men, Marvilla de Las Espinafre's perfervid and exalted nature kept her little circle in constant awe, and she would be often jealous of the Forests (chiefly scrub) which her husband, in his official capacity, was called upon to survey. " Don't lie to me. I know it! You've been to the woods." And after his inspection of the aromatic groves of Lograno, Phædra in full fury tearing her pillow with her teeth was nothing to Marvilla. " Why, dear? Because you've been *among the Myrtles*," was the explanation she chose to give for severing conjugal relations.

"Vittorio forbids the circus on account of germs," the wife of the President of the National Society of Public Morals murmured momentously.

"Really, with this ghastly Boheara, I shall not be grieved when the time comes to set out for dear Santander!" a woman with dog-rose cheeks, and puffed, wrinkled eyes, exclaimed, focusing languishingly the Cardinal.

"He is delicious in handsomeness to-night!"

"A shade battered. But a lover's none the worse in my opinion for acquiring technique," the Duchess of Sarmento declared.

"A lover; what? His Eminence . . .? ?"

The duchess tittered.

"Why not? I expect he has a little woman to whom he takes off his clothes," she murmured, turning to admire the wondrous *Madonna of the Mule-mill* attributed to Murillo.

On a wall-sofa just beneath, crowned with flowers and aigrettes, sat Conca, Marchioness of Macarnudo.

"*Que tal?*"

"My joie de vivre is finished; still, it's amazing how I go on!" the Marchioness answered, making a corner for the duchess. She had known her "dearest Luiza" since the summer the sun melted the church bells and their rakish, pleasure-loving, affectionate hearts had dissolved together. But this had not been yesterday; no; for the Marchioness was a *grandmother* now.

"Conca, Conca: one sees you're in love."

"He's from *Avila*, dear—the footman."

"What!"

"Nothing *classic*—but, oh!"

"Fresh and blonde? I've seen him."

"Such sep . . ."

"Santiago be praised!"

The Marchioness of Macarnudo plied her fan.

"Our hands first met at table . . . yes, dear; but what I always say is, one spark explodes the mine!" And with a sigh she glanced rhapsodically at her fingers, powdered and manicured and encrusted with rings. "Our hands met first at table," she repeated.

"And . . . and the rest?" the duchess gasped.

"I sometimes wish, though, I resembled my sister more, who cares only for amorous, 'delicate' men— the Claudes, so to speak. But there it is! And, any-way, dear," the Marchioness dropped her voice, "he keeps me from thinking (ah perhaps more than I should) of my little grandson. Imagine, Luiza . . . Fifteen, white and vivid rose, and ink-black hair. . . ." And the Marchioness cast a long, pencilled eye towards the world-famous Pietà above her head. "Queen of Heaven, defend a weak woman from *that!*" she besought.

Surprised, and considerably edified, by the sight of the dowager in prayer, Mother Saint-Mary-of-the-Angels was emboldened to advance: The lovely, self-willed donkey (or was it a mule?) that Our Lady was prodding, one could almost stroke it, hear it bray. . . .

Mother Saint-Mary-of-the-Angels could have almost laughed.

But the recollection of the presence of royalty steadied her.

Behind pink lowered portières it had retired, escorted by the mistress of the house. She wore a gown of ivory-black with heavy golden roses and a few of her large diamonds of ceremony.

"I love your Englishy-Moorishy cosy comfort, Decima, and I love——" the Princess Aurora had started to rave.

"An hyperæsthesia injection? . . . a beaten egg?" her hostess solicitously asked.

"*Per caritad!*" the Princess fluted, stooping to

examine a voluptuous small *terre cuite*, depicting a pair of hermaphrodites amusing themselves.

She was looking like the ghost in the Ballet of Ghislaine, after an unusually sharp touch of Boheara; eight-and-forty hours in bed, and, scandal declared, not alone.

" A Cognac? . . . a crême de Chile? . . ."

" Nothing, nothing," the Princess negligently answered, sweeping her long, primrose trailing skirts across the floor.

It was the boudoir of the Winterhalters and Isabeys, once the bright glory of the Radziwollowna collection, which, after several decades of disesteem, were returning to fashion and favour.

" And I love——" she broke off, nearly stumbling over an old blind spaniel, that resided in a basket behind the " supposed original " of the *Lesbia of Lysippus*.

" Clapsey, Clapsey! " her mistress admonished. The gift of a dear and once intimate friend, the dog seemed inclined to outlive itself and become a nuisance.

Alas, poor, fawning Clapsey! Fond, toothless bitch. Return to your broken doze, and dream again of leafy days in leafy Parks, and comfy drives and escapades long ago. What sights you saw when you could see; fountains, and kneeling kings, and grim beggars at Church doors (those at San Eusebio were the worst). And sheltered spas by glittering seas: Santander! And dark adulteries and dim woods at night.

" And I love your Winterhalters! "

Beneath one of these, like a red geranium, was Cardinal Pirelli.

" Oh, your Eminence, the utter forlornness of Society! . . . Besides, (oh, my God!) to be the *one* Intellectual of a Town . . ." a wizened little woman, mistaken, not infrequently, for " Bob Foy," the jockey, was exclaiming plaintively.

" I suppose? " Monseigneur nodded. He was looking rather Richelieu, draped in ermines and some old lace of a beautiful fineness.

" It's pathetic how entertaining is done now. Each year meaner. There was a time when the DunEdens gave balls, and one could count, as a rule, on supper. To-night, there's nothing but a miserable Buffet, with flies trimming themselves on the food; and the champagne that I tasted, well, I can assure your Eminence it was more like foul flower-water than Mumm."

" Disgraceful," the Cardinal murmured, surrendering with suave dignity his hand to the lips of a pale youth all mouchoir and waist.

These kisses of young men, ravished from greedy Royalty, had a delicate savour.

The One Intellectual smiled obliquely.

" Your Eminence I notice has several devout salve-stains already," she murmured, defending her face with her fan.

" Believe me, not all these imprints were left by men! "

The One Intellectual glanced away.

" The poor Princess! I ask you, has one the right to look *so* dying? "

" Probably not," the Cardinal answered, following her ethereal transit.

It was the turn of the tide, and soon admittance to the boudoir had ceased causing " heartburnings."

Nevertheless some few late sirens were only arriving.

Conspicuous among these was Catherine (the ideal-questing, God-groping and insouciant), Countess of Constantine, the aristocratic heroine of the capital, looking half-charmed to be naked and alive. Possessing but indifferent powers of conversation—at Tertulias and dinners she seldom shone—it was yet she who had coined that felicitous phrase: *Some men's eyes are sweet to rest in.*

28

Limping a little, since she had sprained her foot, alas, while turning backward somersaults to a negro band in the black ballroom of the Infanta Eulalia-Irene, her reappearance after the misadventure was a triumph.

"Poor Kitty: it's a shame to ask her, if it's not a ball!" the Inspector of Rivers and Forests exclaimed, fondling the silvery branches of his moustache.

But, at least, a Muse, if not musicians, was at hand.

Clasping a large bouquet of American Beauty-roses, the Poetess Diana Beira Baixa was being besieged by admirers, to " give them something; just something! *Anything* of her own." Wedded, and proclaiming (*in vers libres*) her lawful love, it was whispered she had written a pæan to her husband's " ... " beginning *Thou glorious wonder!* which was altogether too conjugal and intimate for recitation in society.

" They say I utter the cry of sex throughout the Ages, " she murmured, resting her free hand idly on a table of gold and lilac lacquer beside her.

The Duchess-Dowager of Vizeu spread prudishly her fan.

"Since me maid set me muskito net afire, I'm just a bunch, me dear, of hysterics, " she declared.

But requests for "something; just something!" were becoming insistent, and indeed the Muse seemed about to comply when, overtaken by the first alarming symptoms of "Boheara," she fell with a long-drawn sigh to the floor.

V I

REPAIRING the vast armholes of a chasuble, Madame Poco, the venerable Superintendent-of-the-palace, considered, as she worked, the social status of a Spy. It was not without a fleeting qualm that she had crossed the borderland that divides mere curiosity from professional vigilance, but having succumbed to the profitable proposals of certain monsignori, she had grown as keen on her quarry as a tigress on the track.

" It's a wearing life you're leading me, Don Alvaro; but I'll have you," she murmured, singling out a thread.

For indeed the Higher-curiosity is inexorably exacting, encroaching, all too often, on the hours of slumber and rest.

" It's not the door-listening," she decided, " so much as the garden, and, when he goes awenching, the Calle Nabuchodonosor."

She was seated by an open window, commanding the patio and the gate.

" *Vamos, vamos!* " Madame Poco sighed, her thoughts straying to the pontifical supremacy of Tertius II, for already she was the Pope's Poco, his devoted Phœbe, his own true girl: " I'm true blue, dear. True blue."

Forgetful of her needle, she peered interestedly on her image in a mirror on the neighbouring wall. It was a sensation of pleasant novelty to feel between her skull and her mantilla the notes of the first instalment of her bribe.

" Earned, every *perra gorda*, earned! " she exclaimed, rising and pirouetting in elation before the glass.

Since becoming the courted favourite of the chapter, she had taken to strutting-and-languishing in private before her mirror, improvising occult dance-steps, semi-sacred in character, modelled on those of Felix Ganay at White Easter, all in the flowery Spring. Ceremonial poses such as may be observed in storied-windows and olden *pietas* in churches (Dalilaesque, or Shulamitish, as the case might be) were her especial delight, and from these had been evolved an eerie " Dance of Indictment."

Finger rigid, she would advance ominously with slow, Salomé-like liftings of the knees upon a phantom Cardinal: " And thus I accuse thee! " or " I denounce thee, Don Alvaro, for," etc.

" *Dalila!* You old sly gooseberry," she chuckled, gloating on herself in the greenish-spotted depth of a tall, time-corroded glass.

Punch and late hours had left their mark.

" All this Porto and stuff to keep awake make a woman liverish," she commented, examining critically her tongue.

It was a Sunday evening of *corrida*, towards the Feast of Corpus, and through the wide-open window came the near sound of bells.

Madame Poco crossed and recrossed her breast.

They were ringing " Paula," a bell which, tradition said, had fused into its metal one of the thirty pieces of silver received by the Iscariot for the betrayal of Christ.

" They seem to have asked small fees in those days," she reflected, continuing her work.

It was her resolution to divide her reward between masses for herself and the repose and " release " (from Purgatory) of her husband's soul, while anything over should be laid out on finery for a favourite niece, the little Leonora, away in the far Americas.

Madame Poco plied pensively her needle.

She was growing increasingly conscious of the physical demands made by the Higher-curiosity upon a constitution already considerably far-through, and the need of an auxiliary caused her to regret her niece. More than once, indeed, she had been near the point of asking Charlotte Chiemsee, the maid of the Duchess of Vizeu, to assist her. It was Charlotte who had set the duchess's bed-veils on fire while attempting to nip a romance.

But alone and unaided it was astonishing the evidence Madame Poco had gained, and she smiled, as she sewed, at the recollection of her latest capture—the handkerchief of Luna Sainz.

" These hennaed heifers that come to confess! . . . " she scoffed sceptically. For Madame Poco had some experience of men—those brown humbugs (so delicious in tenderness)—in her time. " Poor soul! He had the prettiest teeth . . ." she murmured, visualising forlornly her husband's face. He had been coachman for many years to the sainted Countess of Triana, and he would tell the story of the pious countess and the vermin she had turned to flowers of flame while foraging one day among some sacks before a second-hand-clothes shop. It was she, too, who on another occasion, had changed a handful of marsh-slush into fine slabs of chocolate, each slab engraved with the insignia of a Countess and the sign of the Cross.

" Still, she didn't change *him*, though! " Madame Poco reflected dryly, lifting the lid to her work-box.

Concealed among its contents was a copy of the gay and curious *Memoirs of Mlle. Emma Crunch*, so famous as " Cora Pearl ";—a confiscated bedside-book once belonging to the Cardinal-Archbishop.

" Ps, ps! " she purred, feeling amorously for her scissors beneath the sumptuous oddments of old church velvet and brocade that she loved to ruffle and ruck.

" Ps."

She had been freshening a little the chasuble worn last by his Eminence at the baptism of the blue-eyed police-pup of the Duquesa DunEden, which bore still the primrose trace of an innocent insult.

"A disgraceful business altogether," Madame Poco sighed.

Not everyone knew the dog was christened in *white menthe.* . . .

" Sticky stuff," she brooded: "and a liqueur I never cared for! It takes a lot to beat aniseed brandy; when it's old. Manzanilla runs it close; but it's odd how a glass or two turns me muzzy."

She remained a moment lost in idle reverie before the brilliant embroideries in her basket. Bits of choice beflowered brocade, multi-tinted, inimitably faded silks of the epoca of Theresa de Ahumada, exquisite tatters, telling of the Basilica's noble past, it gladdened the eyes to gaze on. What garden of Granada could show a pink to match that rose, or what sky show a blue as tenderly serene as that azure of the Saint Virgin?

" *Vamos*," she exclaimed, rising: "it's time I took a toddle to know what he's about."

She had last seen the Cardinal coming from the orange orchard with a dancing-boy and Father Fadrique, who had a mark on his cheek left by a woman's fan.

Her mind still dwelling on men (those divine humbugs), Madame Poco stepped outside.

Traversing a white-walled corridor, with the chasuble on her arm, her silhouette, illumined by the splendour of the evening sun, all but caused her to start.

It was in a wing built in the troublous reign of Alfonso the Androgyne that the vestments were kept. Whisking by a decayed and ancient painting, representing " Beelzebub " at Home, she passed slowly through a little closet supposed to be frequented by the ghosts of evil persons long since dead. Just off it was the vestry, gay with blue azulejos tiles of an admirable lustre.

They were sounding Matteo now, a little bell with a passionate voice.

" The pet! " Madame Poco paused to listen. She had her " favourites " among the bells, and Matteo was one of them. Passiaflora, too—but Anna, a light slithery bell, " like a housemaid in hysterics," offended her ear by lack of tone; Sebastian, a complaining, excitable bell, was scarcely better,—" a fretful lover!" She preferred old " Wanda " the Death-bell, a trifle monotonous, and fanatical perhaps, but " interesting," and opening up vistas to varied thought and speculation.

Lifting a rosary from a linen-chest, Madame Poco laid the chasuble within. It was towards this season she would usually renew the bags of bergamot among the Primate's robes.

" This espionage sets a woman all behindhand," she commented to Tobit, the vestry cat.

Black as the Evil One, perched upon a Confessional's ledge, cleansing its belly, the sleek thing sat.

It was the " ledge of forgotten fans," where privileged Penitents would bring their tales of vanity, infidelity and uncharitableness to the Cardinal once a week.

" Directing half-a-dozen duchesses must be frequently a strain! " Madame Poco deliberated, picking up a discarded mitre and trying it absently on.

With a plume at the side or a cluster of balls, it would make quite a striking toque, she decided, casting a fluttered glance on the male effigy of a pale-faced member of the Quesada family, hewn in marble by the door.

Caramba! I thought it was the Cardinal; it gave

34

me quite a turn," she murmured, pursuing lightly her way.

Being a Sunday evening of corrida, it was probable the Cardinal had mounted to his aerie, to enjoy the glimpse of Beauty returning from the fight.

Oh, mandolines of the South, warm throats, and winged songs, winging . . .

Following a darkened corridor with lofty windows closely barred, Madame Poco gained an ambulatory, terminated by a fresco of Our Lady, ascending to heaven in a fury of paint.

"These damp flags'll be the death of me," she complained, talking with herself, turning towards the garden.

Already the blue pushing shadows were beguiling from the shelter of the cloister eaves the rueful owls. A few flittermice, too, were revolving around the long apricot chimneys of the Palace, that, towards sunset, looked like the enchanted castle of some sleeping Princess.

"Bits of pests," she crooned, taking a neglected alley of old bay-tree laurels, presided over by a plashing fountain comprised of a Cupid sneezing. Wary of mole-hills and treacherous roots, she roamed along, preceded by the floating whiteness of a Persian peacock, mistrustful of the intentions of a Goat-sucker owl. Rounding a sequestered garden seat, beneath an aged cypress, the bark all scented knots, Madame Poco halted.

Kneeling before an altar raised to the cult of Our Lady of Dew, Cardinal Pirelli was plunged in prayer.

"Salve. Salve Regina. . . ." Above the tree-tops a bird was singing.

VII

THE College of Noble Damosels in the Calle Santa
Fé was in a whirl. It was " Foundation " day, an event
annually celebrated with considerable fanfaronade
and social éclat. Founded during the internecine wars
of the Middle Age, the College, according to early
records, had suffered rapine on the first day of term.
Hardly, it seemed, had the last scholar's box been
carried upstairs than a troop of military had made its
appearance at the Pension gate demanding, with
"male peremptoriness," a billet. " I, alone," the
Abbess ingeniously states, in relating the poignant
affair in her unpublished diary: " I alone did all I was
able to keep them from them, for which they (the
scholars) called me ' greedy.' " Adding, not without
a touch of modern socialism in disdain for titles, that
she had preferred " the staff-officers to the Field-
Marshal," while as to ensigns, in her estimation, why,
" one was worth the lot."

Polishing urbanely her delicate nails, the actual
President, a staid, pale woman with a peacock nose,
recalled the chequered past. She hoped his Eminence
when he addressed the girls, on handing them their
prizes, would refer to the occasion with all the tact-
fulness required.

" When I think of the horrid jokes the old Marqués
of Illescas made last year," she murmured, bestowing
a harrowed smile on a passing pupil.

She was ensconced in a ponderous fauteuil of figured
velvet (intended for the plump posterior of Royalty)
beneath the incomparable " azulejos " ceiling of
the Concert-room, awaiting the return of Madame

Always Alemtejo, the English governess, from the printers, in the Plaza de Jesus, with the little silver-printed programmes (so like the paste-board cards of brides!), which, as usual, were late.

"Another year we'll type them," she determined, awed by the ardent tones of a young girl rehearsing an aria from the new opera, *Leda*—"Gaze not on Swans."

"Ah, gaze not so on Swan-zzz! . . ."

"Crisper, child. Distinction. Don't exaggerate," the President enjoined, raising a hand to the diamonds on her heavy, lead-white cheeks.

Née an Arroyolo, and allied by marriage with the noble house of Salvaterra, the head mistress in private life was the Dowager-Marchioness of Pennisflores.

"*Nosotros*, you know, are not candidates for the stage! Bear in mind your moral," she begged, with a lingering glance at her robe of grey georgette.

The word "moral," never long from the President's lips, seemed, with her, to take on an intimate tinge, a sensitiveness of its own. She would invest the word at times with an organic significance, a mysterious dignity, that resembled an avowal made usually only in solemn confidence to a doctor or a priest.

The severity of my moral. The prestige of my moral. The perfection of my moral. She has no dignity of moral. I fear a person of no positive moral. Nothing to injure the freshness of her moral. A difficulty of moral. The etiquette of my moral. The majesty of my moral, etc., etc.—as uttered by the President, became, psychologically, interesting *dicta*.

"Beware of a facile moral!" she added, for the benefit of the singer's accompanist, a young nun with a face like some strange white rock, who was inclined to give herself married airs, since she had been debauched, one otiose noon, by a demon.

37

"Ah, Madame Always." The President swam to meet her.

British born, hailing from fairy Lisbon, Madame Always Alemtejo seemed resigned to live and die in a land of hitches.

"The delay is owing to the Printers' strike," she announced. "The Plaza's thronged: the Cigar factory girls, and all the rag-tag and bobtail, from the Alcazaba to the Puerta del Mar, are going out in sympathy, and——"

"The tarts?"

"The t's from Chamont are on the way."

It was the President's custom to lay all vexations before Nostra Señora de los Remedios, the college's divine Protectress, with whose gracious image she was on the closest footing.

Consulting her now as to the concert-programmes, the President recalled that no remedy yet had been found for Señorita Violeta de las Cubas, who had thrown her engagement ring into a place of less dignity than convenience and refused to draw it out.

"Sapphires, my favourite stones," the President reflected, wondering if she should ask "la Inglese" to recover it with the asparagus-tongs.

But already a few *novios*, eager to behold their *novias* again, were in the Patio beneath the "Heiresses' Wing," exciting the connoisseurship of a bevy of early freshness.

"You can tell *that* by his eyebrows!" a girl of thirteen, and just beginning as a woman, remarked.

"*Que barbaridad.*"

"Last summer at Santander Maria-Manuela and I bathed with him, and one morning there was a tremendous sea, with *terrific* waves, and we noticed unmistakably."

"I can't explain; but I adore all that mauvishness about him!"

" I prefer Manolito to Gonzalito, though neither thrill me like the Toreador Tancos."

Assisted by Fräulein Pappenheim and Muley, the President's negress maid, they were putting the final touches to their vestal frocks.

" Men are my raging disgust," a florid girl of stupendous beauty declared, saturating with a flacon of *Parfum cruel* her prematurely formed silhouette.

" Nsa, nsa, señorita," Muley mumbled. " Some know better dan dat! "

" To hell with them! "

" *Adios*, Carlo. *Adios*, Juan. Join you down dah in one minute." The negress chuckled jauntily.

" Muley, Muley," Fräulein chided.

" What wonder next I 'bout to hear? "

Delighting in the tender ferocities of Aphrodite, she was ever ready to unite the *novio* to the *novia*. For window-vigils (where all is hand play) few could contrive more ingeniously than she those fans of fresh decapitated flowers, tuberose punctuated with inebriating jasmine, so beloved in the East by the dark children of the sun. Beyond Cadiz the blue, the beautiful, in palm-girt Marrakesh, across the sea, she had learnt other arts besides. . . .

" Since seeing Peter Prettylips on the screen the Spanish type means nothing to me," Señorita Soledad, a daughter of the first Marqués of Belluga, the greatest orange-king in the Peninsula, remarked.

" How low. She is not noble."

" I *am* noble."

" Oh no; you're not."

" Cease wrangling," Fräulein exclaimed, " and enough of that," she added sharply, addressing a *novio*less little girl looking altogether bewitching of naughtiness as she tried her ablest to seduce by her crude manœuvres the fiancé of a friend. Endowed with the lively temperament of her grandmother,

39

Conca, Marchioness of Macarnudo, the impressionable, highly amative nature of the little Obdulia gave her governesses some grounds for alarm. At the Post Office one day she had watched a young man lick a stamp. His rosy tongue had vanquished her. In fact, at present, she and a class-chum, Milagros, were " collecting petals " together—and much to the bewilderment of those about them, they might be heard on occasion to exclaim, at Mass, or in the street: " Quick, did you see it? " " No." " Santissima! *I* did! "

" Shrimp. As if Gerardo would look at her! " his *novia* scoffed. " But let me tell you, young woman," she turned upon the shrinking Obdulia, " that social ostracism, and even, in certain cases " (she slapped and pinched her), " *assassination* attends those that thieve or tamper with another's lover! And Fräulein will correct me if I exaggerate."

Fräulein Pappenheim was a little woman already drifting towards the sad far shores of forty, with no experience of the pains of Aphrodite caused by men; only at times she would complain of stomach aches in the head.

" Dat is so," Muley struck in sententiously for her. " Dair was once a young lady ob Fez——"

But from the Patio the college chaplain, Father Damien Forment, known as " Shiny-nose," was beckoning to the heiresses to join their relatives in the reception-hall below.

Since that sanguinary period of Christianity, synchronising with the foundation of the institution of learning in the Calle Santa Fé, what changes in skirts and trousers the world has seen. Alone unchanging are women's ambitions and men's desires.

" Dear child. . . . She accepts him . . . but a little à contre-cœur," the President was saying to the Marchioness of las Cubas, an impoverished society belle, who went often without bread in order to buy lip-sticks and rouge.

" With Violeta off my hands . . . Ah, President, if only Cecilio could be suitably *casada*."

" In my little garden I sometimes work a brother. The heiresses' windows are all opening to the flowers and trees. . . . The boy should be in polo kit. A uniform interests girls," the President murmured, turning with an urbane smile to welcome the Duquesa DunEden.

She had a frock of black kasha, signed Paul Orna, with a cluster of brown-and-pink orchids, like sheep's-kidneys, and a huge feather hat.

" I'm here for my God-girl, Gloria," she murmured, glancing mildly round.

Incongruous that this robust, rich woman should have brought to the light of heaven no heir, while the unfortunate Marchioness, needy, and frail of physique, a wraith, did not know what to do with them!

The President dropped a sigh.

She was prepared to take a dog of the daughterless Duquesa. A bitch, of course. . . . But let it be Police, or Poodle! It would lodge with the girls. A cubicle to itself in the heiresses' wing; and since there would be no extra class-charge for dancing or drawing, no course *in belli arti*, some reduction of fees might be arranged. . . . " We would turn her out a creature of breeding. . . . An eloquent tail-wave, a disciplined moral, and with a reverence moreover for house-mats and carpets." The President decided to draw up the particulars of the prospectus by and by.

" Your Goddaughter is quite one of our most promising exhibitioners," she exclaimed, indicating with her fan some water-colour studies exposed upon the walls.

" She comes of a mother with a mania for painting,"

the Duquesa declared, raising a lorgnon, critically, before the portrait of a Lesbian, with dying, fabulous eyes.

" Really? "

" A positive passion," the Duquesa answered, with a swift, discerning glance at an evasive " nude," showing the posterior poudrederizé of a Saint.

" I had no idea," the President purred, drawing attention to a silvery streetscape.

" It's the Rambla from the back of Our Lady of the Pillar! It was rare fun doing it, on account of the *pirapos* of the passers-by," the artist, joining them, explained.

" Dear child, I predict for her a great deal of admiration very soon," the President murmured, with a look of reproach at a youthful pupil as she plied her boy-Father with embarrassing questions: " Who are the chief society women in the moon? What are their names? Have they got motor-cars there? Is there an Opera-House? Are there bulls? "

The leering aspect of a lady in a costume of blonde Guadalmedina lace and a hat wreathed with clipped black cocks' feathers arrested her.

Illusion-proof, with a long and undismayed service in Love's House (sorry brutes, all the same, though, these men, with their selfishness, fickleness and lies!) the Marchioness of Macarnudo with her mysterious " legend " (unscrupulous minxes, all the same, though, these women, with their pettiness, vanity and . . .!), was too temperamentally intriguing a type to be ignored.

" Isn't that little Marie Dorothy with the rosebuds stuck all over her? " she asked her granddaughter, who was teasing her brother on his moustache.

" To improve the growth, the massage of a *novia's* hand," she fluted, provoking the marchioness to an involuntary nervous gesture. Exasperated by resistance, struggling against an impossible infatuation, her Spanish ladyship was becoming increasingly subject to passing starts. Indeed only in excitement and dissipation could her unsatisfied longings find relief. Sometimes she would run out in her car to where the men bathe at Ponte Delgado, and one morning, after a ball, she had been seen standing on the main road to Cadiz in a cabuchon tiara, watching the antics of some nude muleteers: *Black as young Indians*—she had described them later.

" My sweet butterfly! What next? " she exclaimed, ogling Obdulia, whose elusive resemblance to her brother was really curiously disturbing.

Averting a filmy eye, she recognised Marvilla de las Espinafres, airing anti-patriotic views on birth control, her arms about an adopted daughter. " Certainly not; most decidedly *no!* I should scream! " she was saying as from the Concert-room the overture began thinning the crowd.

" It's nothing else than a national disaster," the marchioness declared to her grandson, " how many women nowadays seem to shirk their duty! "

" Well, the de las Cubas hasn't, anyway," he demurred.

" Poor thing. They say she jobs her mules," the marchioness murmured, exchanging a nod with the passing President.

Something, manifestly, had occurred to disturb the equilibrium of her moral.

" Such a disappointment, *Nostra Señora!* " she exclaimed. " Monseigneur, it seems, has thrown me over."

" Indeed; how awkward! "

" I fear though even more so for his chapter."

" He is not ill? "

" *Cardinal Pirelli has fled the capital!* "

VIII

Standing amid gardens made for suffering and delight is the disestablished and, *sic transit*, slowly decaying monastery of the Desierto. Lovely as Paradise, oppressive perhaps as Eden, it had been since the days of the mystic Luigi of Granada a site well suited to meditation and retreat. Here, in the stilly cypress-court, beneath the snowy sierras of Santa Maria la Blanca, Theresa of Avila, worn and ill, though sublime in laughter, exquisite in beatitude, had composed a part of the *Way of Perfection*, and, here, in these same realms of peace, dominating the distant city of Clemenza and the fertile plains of Andalucia, Cardinal Pirelli, one blue mid-day towards the close of summer, was idly considering his Defence. "*Apologia*, no; merely a defence," he mused: " merely," he flicked the ash-tip of a cigar, " a defence! I defend myself, that's all! . . ."

A sigh escaped him.

Divided by tranquil vineyards and orange-gardens from the malice and vindictiveness of men it was difficult to experience emotions other than of forgiveness and love.

" Come, dears, and kiss me," he murmured, closing consentingly his eyes.

It was the forgetful hour of noon, when Hesperus from his heavens confers on his pet Peninsula the boon of sleep.

" A nice nap he's having, poor old gentleman." Madame Poco surveyed her master.

Ill at ease and lonely in the austere dismantled house, she would keep an eye on him at present almost as much for company as for gain.

44

As handsome and as elegant as ever, his physiognomy in repose revealed a thousand strange fine lines, suggestive subtleties, intermingled with less ambiguous signs, denoting stress and care.

"He's growing almost huntedish," she observed, casting a brief glance at the literature beside him—The Trial of Don Fernando de la Cerde, Bishop of Barcelona, defrocked for putting young men to improper uses; a treatise on The Value of Smiles; an old volume of Songs, by Sà de Miranda; The Lives of Five Negro Saints, from which escaped a bookmark of a dancer in a manton.

"Everything but his Breviary," she commented, perceiving a soutaned form through the old flowered ironwork of the courtyard gateway.

Regretting her better gown of hooped watered-silk, set aside while in retreat (for economy's sake), Madame Poco fled to put it on, leaving the visitor to announce himself.

The padre of Our Lady of the Valley, the poor padre of Our Lady, would the Primate know? Oh, every bird, every rose, could have told him that: the padre of Our Lady bringing a blue trout for his Eminence's supper from the limpid waters of Lake Orense.

Respecting the Primate's rest Father Felicitas, for so, also, was he named, sat down discreetly to await his awakening.

It was a rare sweetness to have the Cardinal to himself thus intimately. Mostly, in the city, he would be closely surrounded. Not that Father Felicitas went very much to town; no; he disliked the confusion of the streets, and even the glories of the blessed basilicas made him scarcely amends for the quiet shelter of his hills.

The blessed basilicas, you could see them well from here. The giralda of Saint Xarifa, and the august twin towers of the cathedral, and the azulejos dome of Saint Eusebio, that was once a pagan mosque; while of Santissima Marias, Maria del Carmen, Maria del Rosario, Maria de la Soledad, Maria del Dolores, Maria de las Nieves, few cities in all the wide world could show as many.

"To be sure, to be sure," he exclaimed absently, lifting his eyes to a cloudlet leisurely pointing above the lofty spur of the Pico del Mediodia. "To be sure," he added, seeking to descry the flower-like bellcot of Our Lady of the Valley just beneath.

But before he had discovered it, half concealed by trees, he was reminded by the sound of a long-drawn, love-sick wail, issuing out of the very entrails of the singer, of the lad left in charge of his rod by the gate.

"On the Bridge to Alcantara."

With its protracted cadences and doleful, vain-yearning reaches, the voice, submerged in all the anguish of a Malagueña, troubled, nostalgically, the stillness.

God's will be done. It was enough to awaken the Primate. Not everyone relished a Malagueña, a dirgeful form of melody introduced, tradition said, and made popular in the land, long, long ago, beneath the occupation of the Moors.

Father Felicitas could almost feel the sin of envy as he thought of the flawless choir and noble triumphal organ of the cathedral yonder.

Possessed of no other instrument, Our Lady of the Valley depended at present on a humble guitar. Not that the blessed guitar, with its capacity for emotion, is unworthy to please God's listening ear, but Pepe, the lad appointed to play it, would fall all too easily into those Jotas, Tangos, and Cuban Habaneiras, learnt in wayside fondas and fairs. Some day, Father Felicitas did not doubt, Our Lady would have an organ, an organ with pipes. He had prayed for it so

46

often; oh, so often; and once, quite in the late of twilight while coming through the church, he had seen her, it seemed, standing just where it should be. It had been as though a blinding whiteness.

" A blinding whiteness," he murmured, trembling a little at the recollection of the radiant vision.

Across the tranquil court a rose-red butterfly pursued a blue. " I believe the world is all love, only no one understands," he meditated, contemplating the resplendent harvest plains steeped in the warm sweet sunlight.

" My infinite contrition! " The Cardinal spoke.

A rare occurrence in these days was a visitor, and now with authority ebbing, or in the balance at least, it was singular how he felt a new interest in the concerns of the diocese. The birth-rate and the death-rate and the super-rate, which it was to be feared that the Cortès——

Sailing down the courtyard in her watered-silken gown, Madame Poco approached with Xeres and Manzanilla, fresh from the shuttered snowery or nieveria.

" And I've just buried a bottle of champagne, in case your Eminence should want it," she announced as she inviolably withdrew.

" As devoted a soul as ever there was, and loyal to all my interests," the Primate exclaimed, touched.

" God be praised! "

" An excellent creature," the Cardinal added, focusing on the grey high road beyond the gate two youths on assback, seated close.

"Andalucians, though of another parish."

" I should like much to visit my diocese again; it's some while since I did," the Cardinal observed, filling the Padre's glass.

" You'd find up at Sodré a good many changes."

" Have they still the same little maid at the Posada de la Melodia? "

" Carmencita? "

" A dainty thing."

" She went Therewards about the month of Mary."

" America? It's where they all go."

" She made a ravishing corpse."

" Ahi."

And Doña Beatriz too had died; either in March or May. It was she who would bake the old Greek Sun-bread, and although her heirs had sought high and low no one could find the receipt.

The Cardinal expressed satisfaction.

" Bestemmia," he breathed; " and I trust they never may; for on the Feast of the Circumcision she invariably caused to be laid before the high-altar of the cathedral a peculiarly shaped loaf to the confusion of all who saw it."

And the Alcalde of Ayamonte, Don Deniz, had died on the eve of the bachelors' party he usually gave when he took off his winter beard.

" Ahi; this death . . ."

Ah, yes, and since the delicacies ordered by the corpse could not well be countermanded they had been divided among Christ's poor.

Left to himself once more Cardinal Pirelli returned reluctantly to his Defence.

Half the diocese it seemed had gone " Therewards," while the rest were at Biarritz or Santander. . . .

" A nice cheery time this is! " he murmured, oppressed by the silent cypress-court. Among the blue, pointing shadows, a few frail oleanders in their blood-rose ruby invoked warm brief life and earth's desires.

" A nice cheery time," he repeated, rising and going within.

The forsaken splendour of the vast closed cloisters seemed almost to augur the waning of a cult. Likewise the decline of Apollo, Diana, Isis, with the gradual downfall of their Temples, had been heralded, in past times, by the dispersal of their priests. It looked as though Mother Church, like Venus or Diana, was making way in due turn for the beliefs that should follow: " and we shall begin again with intolerance, martyrdom and converts," the Cardinal ruminated, pausing before an ancient fresco depicting the eleven thousand virgins, or as many as there was room for.

Playing a lonely ball game against them was the disrespectful Chicklet.

" Young vandal," the Cardinal chided, caressing the little acolyte's lustrous locks.

" Monseigneur? . . ."

" There: run along; and say a fragrant prayer for me, Child."

Flinging back a shutter drawn fast against the sun, the boundless prospect from the balcony of his cell recalled the royal Escorial. The white scattered terraces of villas set in dark deeps of trees, tall palms, and parasol-pines so shady, and, almost indistinguishable, the white outline of the sea, made insensibly for company.

Changing into a creation of dull scarlet crêpe, a cobweb dubbed " summer-exile," Cardinal Pirelli felt decidedly less oppressed. " Madrid is on the Manzanares," he vociferated, catching sight of the diligence from Sodré. Frequently it would bring Frasquito, the postman—a big tawny boy, overgiven to passing the day in the woods with his gun and his guitar.

" The mail bag is most irregular," he complained, fastening a few dark red, almost black, roses to his cincture. It was Cardinal Pirelli's fancy while in retreat to assume his triple-Abraham, or mitre, and with staff in hand to roam abroad as in the militant Springtide of the Church.

" When kings were cardinals," he murmured quietly as he left the room.

It was around the Moorish water-garden towards shut of day he liked most to wander, seeking like some Adept to interpret in the still deep pools the mirrored music of the sky.

All, was it vanity? These pointing stars and spectral leaning towers, this mitre, this jewelled ring, these trembling hands, these sweet reflected colours, white of daffodil and golden rose. All, was it vanity?

Circling the tortuous paths like some hectic wingless bird, he was called to the refectory by the tintinnabulation of a bell.

In the deep gloominous room despoiled of all splendour but for a dozen old Zurbarans flapping in their frames, a board, set out with manifest care, was prepared for the evening meal.

Serving both at Mass and table, it was the impish Chicklet who, with a zealous napkin-flick (modelled on the *mozos* of the little café-cum-restaurant " As in Ancient Andalucia " patronised by rising toreadors and *aficianados* of the Ring), showed the Primate to his chair.

Having promised José the chef a handsome indulgence, absolved him from bigamy, and raised his wages, Cardinal Pirelli, in gastronomy nothing if not fastidious, had succeeded in inducing him to brave the ghostly basements of the monastery on the mount.

Perhaps of the many charges brought against the Primate by his traducers, that of making the sign of the cross with his left foot at meals was the most utterly unfounded—looking for a foot-cushion would have been nearer the truth.

Addressing the table briefly in the harmonious Latin tongue, his Eminence sat down with an impenetrable sigh.

With vine-sprays clinging languorously to the candle-stands, rising from a bed of nespoles, tulips, and a species of wild orchid known as Devil's-balls, the Chicklet, to judge from his floral caprices, possessed a little brain of some ambition, not incapable of excess.

"I thought you were tired of jasmine, sir, and th'orange bloom's getting on," he chirruped, coming forward with a cup of cold, clear consommé, containing hearts, coronets and most of the alphabet in vermicelli.

"I'm tired, true, child; but not of jasmine," the Primate returned, following a little contretemps of a marqués' crown, sinking amid a frolicsome bevy of O's.

"I hope it's right, sir?"

"Particularly excellent, child—tell José so."

"Will I bring the trout, sir?"

"Go, boy," the Cardinal bade him, opening a volume by the menu-stand formed of a satyr sentimentalising over a wood-nymph's breasts.

While in retreat it was his fancy, while supping, to pursue some standard work of devotion, such as Orthodoxy so often encourages or allows: it was with just such a golden fairy-tale as this that he had once won a convert: Poor woman. What had become of her? Her enthusiasm, had it lasted? She had been very ardent. Perfervid! "Instruction" would quite wear it out of them. Saint Xarifa's at fall of day; . . . an Autumn affair! Chrysanthemums; big bronze frizzlies. A Mrs. Mandarin Dove. American. Ninety million sterling. Social pride and religious humility, how can I reconcile? The women in Chicago. My God! ! ! My little step-daughter. . . . Her Father, fortunately. . . . Yes, your Eminence, he's dead. And, oh, I'm *glad*. Is it naughty? And then her photograph à la Mary of Magdala, her hair unbound, décolletée, with a dozen long strands of pearls. "Ever penitently yours, Stella Mandarin Dove."

"I'd rather have had the blonde Ambassadress to the Court of St. James," he reflected, toying with the fine table-glass of an old rich glamour. A fluted bell cup sadly chipped provoked a criticism and a citation from Cassiodorus on the " rude " ways of boys.

Revolving around an austere piece of furniture that resembled a Coffin-upon-six-legs, the Chicklet appeared absorbed.

" I hear it's the Hebrew in heaven, sir. Spanish is seldom spoken," he exclaimed seraphically.

" Tut, dear child. Who says so? " the Primate wondered, his eyes wandering in melancholy towards the whitest of moons illumining elusively the room— illumining a long, sexless face with large, mauve, heroic lips in a falling frame, and an " apachey," blue-cheeked Christ, the Cardinal noticed.

" Who, sir? Why, a gentleman I was guide to once!" The Cardinal chuckled comprehensively.

" I should surmise, dear child, there was little to show."

" What, not the crypt, sir? Or the tomb of the beautiful Princess Eboli, the beloved of Philip the Second, sir? "

" Jewel boy. Yum-yum." The Cardinal raised his glass.

" And the bells, sir? Last night, I'll tell you, sir, I thought I heard old ' Wanda ' on the wind."

" Old Wanda, boy."

" She rings for deaths, sir."

" Nonsense, child; your little ears could never hear as far," the Cardinal answered, deliberating if a lad of such alertness and perception might be entrusted to give him a henna shampoo: it was easy enough to remove the towels before it got too red. The difficulty was to apply the henna; evenly everywhere; fair play all round; no favouring the right side more than the left, but golden Justice for each grey hair. Impartiality: proportion! " Fatal, otherwise," the Primate reasoned.

" Are you ready for your Quail, sir? "

" Quail, quail? Bring on the *dulces*, boy," his Eminence murmured, regarding absently through the window the flickering arc-lights of Clemenza far away. Dear beckoning lamps, dear calling lamps; lamps of theatres, cinemas, cabarets, bars and dancings; lamps of railway-termini, and excessively lit hotels, *olé* to you, enchantress lights! "

"And, after all, dears, if I did," the Cardinal breathed, tracing a caricature of his Holiness upon the table-cloth lightly with a dessert-fork. ("Which I certainly deny" . . .), he brooded, disregarding the dissolving Orange ice *à la* Marchioness of Macarnudo."

" Had you anything in the Lottery, sir? "

" Mind your business, boy, and remove this ball-room nastiness," the Primate snapped.

It was while lingering, after dinner, over some choice vintage, that he oftenest would develop the outline of his Defence. To escape the irate horns of the Pontiff's bull (Die, dull beast) he proposed pressing the " Pauline Privilege," unassailable, and confirmed *A.D. 1590* by Pope Sixtus V, home to the battered beauty of the Renaissance hilt. " With the elegance and science," he murmured, " of a *matador*."

" I have the honour to wish you, sir, a good and pleasant night."

" Thanks, boy."

" And if you should want me, sir " . . . the youthful acolyte possessed the power to convey the unuttered.

"If?? . . . And say a fragrant prayer for me, child," the Cardinal enjoined.

Resting an elbow among the nespoles and tulips (dawn-pink and scarlet, awakening sensitively in the candle-glow), he refilled reflectively his glass.

" God's providence is over all," he told himself, considering dreamfully a cornucopia heaped with fruit. Being just then the gracious Autumn, a sweet golden-plum called " Don Jaime of Castile " was in great perfection. It had been for the Southern orchards a singularly fertile year. Never were seen such gaily rouged peaches, such sleek, violet cherries, such immensest white grapes. Nestling delectably amid its long, deeply-lobed leaves, a pomegranate (fruit of joy) attracted the Cardinal's hand.

Its seeds, round and firm as castanets, evoked the Ortiz. " Ah, Jesus-Maria. The evening she waved her breasts at me! " he sighed, attempting to locate the distant lights of the Teatro Trinidades. Interpreting God's world, with her roguish limbs and voice, how witching the child had been but lately in *The Cistus of Venus*. Her valse-refrain " Green Fairy Absinthe " (with a full chorus in tights) had been certainly, theatrically (if, perhaps, not socially), the hit of the season.

" The oleanders come between us," he deliberated, oppressed by the amative complaint of some sweet-throated, summer night-bird.

" It's queer, dears, how I'm lonely! " he exclaimed, addressing the ancient Zurbarans flapping austerely in their frames.

The Archbishop of Archidona, for all his air of pomposity, looked not unsympathetic, neither, indeed, did a little lady with a nimbus, casting melting glances through the spokes of a mystic wheel.

" It's queer—; you'd be surprised! " he murmured, rising and setting an oval moon-backed chair beside his own.

As usual the fanciful watch-dogs in the hills had begun their disquieting barking.

" The evenings are suicide," he ruminated, idly replenishing his glass.

Sometimes, after the fifth or sixth bumper, the great Theresa herself would flit in from the garden. Long had her radiant spirit " walked " the Desierto, seeking, it was supposed, a lost sheet of the manuscript of her *Way of Perfection*. It may have been following on the seventh or even the eighth bumper that the Primate remarked he was not alone.

She was standing by the window in the fluttered moonshine, holding a knot of whitish heliotropes.

" Mother? "

Saint John of the Cross could scarcely have pronounced the name with more wistful ecstasy.

Worn and ill, though sublime in laughter, exquisite in tenderness she came towards him.

" . . . Child? "

" Teach me, oh, teach me, dear Mother, the Way of Perfection."

IX

VERIFYING private dates, revising here and there the cathedral list of charges, Don Moscosco, the secretary of the chapter, seated before his usual bureau, was at the disposal of the public. A ministerial crisis had brought scattered Fashion home to town with a rush, and the pressure of work was enormous. " Business " indeed had seldom been livelier, and chapels for Masses of special intention were being booked in advance as eagerly as opera-boxes for a première, or seaside-villas in the season.

" If the boys are brisk we might work in Joseph," he mused, consulting with closely buttoned lips his Tarifa and plan; " although I'd rather not risk a clash."

Unknown to double-let like his compères on occasion outside, the swarthy little man was a master organiser, never forgetting that the chapter's welfare and prestige were inseparable from his own. Before allotting a chapel for a mass of Intent, it was his rule to analyse and classify the " purity " of the intention (adding five per cent. where it seemed not altogether to be chaste, or where the purpose was " obscure ").

" I see no inconvenience," he murmured, gauging delicately the motif of a couple of great ladies of the bluest blood in Spain who were commissioning masses for the safety of a favourite toreador in an approaching *corrida*.

" Five hundred flambeaux, at least, between them," the secretary, negligently, spat.

It was the twenty-first day of September (which is the Feast of Saint Firmin), and the sacristia, thronged with mantons and monsignorï, resembled some vast shifting parterre of garden-flowers. Having a little altercation together, Mother Mary of the Holy Face and Mother Garcia of the Company of Jesus, alone, seemed stable. In honour of Saint Firmin the door of Pardon (closed half the year) had just been thrown open, bringing from the basilica an odour of burning incense and the strains of a nuptial march.

How many of the bridal guests knew of the coffin installed in the next chapel but one? the little man wondered, rising gallantly to receive a client.

She wore no hat, but a loose veil of gold and purple enveloped her hair and face.

" I fear for him! "

" There, there. What is it? "

" I fear for him "—a man and the stars, nights of sweet love, oleander flowers were in her voice.

By her immense hooped earrings, as large as armlets, he knew her for the Adonira, the mistress of the toreador Tancos.

" Come to me after the Friday miserere," the official objected: " let me entreat an appointment."

" No. Now."

" Well."

" I want a Mass."

" The intention being . . .? " The secretary sent up his brows a little.

" His safety."

" Whose? "

" My lover's."

" But, señorita, it's all done! It's all *done*, dear lady," the words were on Don Moscosco's lips. Still, being the pink of chivalry with *las mujares* and a man of business, he murmured: " With what quantity of lights? "

" Two. Just for him and me."

" Tell me how you would prefer them," he exclaimed, glancing whimsically towards the canvas of the Magdalen waylaying our Lord.

" How I would——" she stammered, opening and closing the fansticks in her painted, love-tired hands.

" You would like them long and, I dare say, gross?"

" The best," she breathed, almost fainting as though from some fleeting delicious vision in the air.

" Leave it to me," Don Moscosco said, and dropping expressively his voice he added: " Come, señorita; won't you make a date with me? "

" A date with you? "

" Ah-hah, the little Juans and Juanas; the charming cherubs! " the secretary archly laughed.

Returning however no answer she moved distractedly away.

" Two tapers! *Two*. As many only as the animal's horns. It's amazing how some women stint," he reflected, faintly nettled.

The marriage ceremony was over. From the summit of the giralda, volley on volley, the vibrant bells proclaimed the consummation.

" It was all so quick; I hope it's valid? " Madame la Horra, the mother of the " Bride," looked in to say. With a rose mole here and a strawberry mole there, men (those adorable monsters) accounted her entirely attractive.

"As *though* we should hurry, as *though* we should clip!"

" Eh? "

" As though we were San Eusebio, or the Pilar! "

" Forgive me, I came only to—I, . . . I, . . . I, . . . I think I cried. The first spring flowers looked so beautiful."

A mother's love, and contrition, perhaps, for her own shortcomings, the secretary brooded. " I shall knock her off five per cent."

Lost in bland speculation Don Moscosco considered the assembly collected outside the curtained *camarin* of the Virgin, where the gowns of the Image were dusted and changed.

For Firmin she usually wore an osprey or two and perfumed ball-gloves of Cordoba, and carried a spread fan of gold Guadalmedina lace. Among devotees of the sacriſtia it was a perpetual wonder to observe how her coſtumes altered her. Sometimes she would appear quite small, dainty and French, at others she would recall the sumptuous women of the Argentine and the New World, and aficionados would lament their fairy isle of Cuba in the far-off Caribbean Sea.

Traversing imperiously the throng, Don Moscosco beheld the Duquesa DunEden.

Despite the optimism of the gazettes it looked as though the Government muſt indeed be tottering, since the Duquesa too was up from her country quinta.

" I have a requeſt to make," she began, sinking gratefully to a chair.

" And charmed, in advance, to grant it."

" I suppose you will have forgotten my old spaniel, Clapsey? "

" Ah, no more dogs! "

" She is passing-out, poor darling; and if the Church could spare her some trifling favour——"

" Impossible."

" She is the firſt toy tail for my little cemetery! "

" Quite impossible."

" Poor pet," the Duquesa exclaimed undaunted: " she has shared in her time my moſt intimate secrets: she ſtands for early memories; what rambles we'd go together, she and I, at Santander long ago! I remember Santander, Don Moscosco (imagine), when there was not even an hotel! A little fishing-village, so quiet, so quiet; ah, it was nicer, far, and more exclusive then. . . ."

" I dare say."

" You know my old, blind and devoted friend was a gift from the king; and this morning I said to her: ' Clapsey! Clapsey! ' I said: ' where's Carlos? Car-los . . . ? ' And I'll take my oath she rallied."

Don Moscosco unbent a shade: " A token, is she, of royalty? "

" He also gave me ' Flirt '! "

" Perhaps a brief mass . . ."

" Poor dearest: you'll keep it quiet and black? "

" We say all but the Black."

" Oh? "

" One must draw the line somewhere! " Don Moscosco declared, his eye roving towards a sacristan piloting a party of travel-stained tourists, anxious to inspect the casket containing a feather from the Archangel Gabriel's wing.

" I know your creative taste! I rely on you," the Duquesa rose remarking.

Nevertheless, beneath the routine of the sacristia the air was surcharged with tension. Rival groups, pro- or anti-Pirellian, formed almost irreconcilable camps, and partisanship ran high. Not a few among the cathedral staff had remained true to his Eminence, and Mother Sunlight, a charwoman (who sometimes performed odd jobs at the Palace), had taught her infant in arms to cry: " Long live Spain and Cardinal Pirelli! "

Enough, according to some extreme anti-Pirellians, to be detrimental to her milk.

" I'm told the Pope has sent for him at last," the laundress of the Basilica, Doña Consolacion, remarked to Sister June of the Way Dolorous.

" Indeed, indeed; it scarcely does to think! "

" Does anyone call to mind a bit of a girl (from Bilbao she was) that came once to stop as his niece?"

" Inclined to a moustache! Perfectly."

" Phœbe Poco protests she wasn't."

" Ah, well; a little *Don Juanism* is good," the laundress said, and sighed.

" She declares . . ."

" She tells the truest lies, dear, of anyone I know! "

" Be that as it may it's certain he's getting increasingly eccentric. But Sunday last, entertaining his solicitor, it seems he ordered coffee after the merienda to be served in two chamber-pots."

" Shameful—and he in his sunset years! " Mother Mary of the Holy Face commented, coming up with Tomás the beadle.

" It wouldn't surprise me," he declared, drowsily shaking a heavy bouquet of keys, " if the thread of his life was about to break."

" *Hombre* . . ." The laundress expressed alarm.

" Often now, towards Angelus, as I climb the tower, I hear the bell Herod talking with old Wanda in the loft. Eeeeeee! Eeeeeee! Horrible things they keep saying. Horrible things they keep saying."

" Nonsense," Doña Consolacion exclaimed, bestowing a smile on Monsignor Cuxa. Old, and did-did-doddery, how frail he seemed beside Father Fadrique, the splendid swagger of whose chasuble every woman must admire.

" Sent for to Rome; ah, sangre mio, I wish someone would send for me," a girl, with a rose in the hair beautifully placed, sighed romantically.

" Be satisfied with Spain, my dear, and remember that no other country can compare with it! " Doña Generosa, an Aunt of one of the cathedral dancing-boys (who drew a small pension as the widow of the late Leader of applause at the Opera-house), remonstrated.

" I've never travelled," Doña Consolacion blandly confessed: " but I dare say, dear, you can't judge of Egypt by *Aïda*."

" Oh, can't I, though? " Doña Generosa sniffed, as the Father of an acolyte raised his voice.

" Spain! " he exclaimed, exalted, throwing a lover's kiss to the air, " Spain! The most glorious country in God's universe, His admitted masterpiece, His gem,

His——" He broke off, his eloquence dashed by the sad music of Monsignor Cuxa's hæmorrhage.

An office in the Chapel of the Crucifix was about to begin, recalling to their duties the scattered employees of the staff.

Hovering by the collection-box for the Souls in Hades, the Moorish maid from the College of Noble Damosels, bound on an errand of trust as ancient as the world, was growing weary of watching the people come and go.

" I must have missed him beneath the trees of the Market Place," she ruminated, straightening on her head a turban wreathed in blossoms.

It was the matter of a message from Obdulia and Milagros to the radiant youth whose lips they were so idyllically (if perhaps somewhat licentiously) sharing.

" Fo' sh'o dis goin' to put dose heiresses in a quandry," she deliberated, oppressed by her surroundings.

Eastern in origin like the Mesquita of Cordoba, it was impossible to forget that the great basilica of Clemenza was a Mosque profaned.

Designed for the cult of Islam, it made her African's warm heart bleed to behold it now. Would it were reconverted to its virginal state, and the cry of the muezzin be heard again summoning men to Muhammad's house! Yes, the restitution of the cathedral to Allah was Muley's cherished dream, and it consoled her, on certain days when she was homesick, to stand before the desecrated mihrab in worship, her face turned towards Africa, and palm-girt Marrakesh across the sea.

" I almost inclined to slip across to de Café Goya," she breathed, moving aside for a shuffling acolyte, bearing a crucifix on a salver.

Led by the pious sisters of the noble order of the Flaming-Hood, the Virgin was returning to her niche.

She was arrayed as though bound for the Bull-ring, in a robe of peacock silk, and a mantilla of black lace.

" *Santissima!* . . ."

" *Elegantissima!* " Devotees dropped adoring to the floor.

Alone, the African remained erect.

" Muhammad mine, how long? " she sighed, turning entreating eyes to the cabbalistic letters and Saracenic tracings of the azulejos arabesques.

X

MIDNIGHT had ceased chiming from the Belfry tower, and the laſt seguidilla had died away. Looking fresh as a rose, and incredibly juvenile in his pyjamas of silver-grey and scarlet (the racing colours of Vittoria, Duchess of Vizeu), the Cardinal seemed disinclined for bed.

Surveying in detachment the preparatives for his journey (set out beneath an El Greco Chriſt, with outspread, delicate hands), he was in the mood to dawdle.

" These for the Frontier. Those for the train," he exclaimed aloud, addressing a phantom porter.

Among the personalia was a passport, the likeness of identity showing him in a mitre, cute to tears, though, essentially, orthodox; a flask of Napoleon brandy, to be " declared " if not consumed before leaving the Peninsula; and a novel, *Self-Essence*, on the Index, or about to be.

" A coin, child, and put them for me on the rack," he enjoined the wraith, regarding through the window the large and radiant ſtars.

The rhythmic murmur of a weeping fountain filled momentously the night.

Its lament evoked the Chicklet's sobs.

" Did I so wrong, my God, to punish him? Was I too haſty? " the Primate asked, repairing towards an ivory crucifix by Cano ; " yet, Thou knoweſt, I adore the boy! "

He paused a moment aſtonished by the revelation of his heart.

" It muſt have been love that made me do it," he

smiled, considering the incident in his mind. Assuredly the rebuff was unpremeditated, springing directly from the boy's behaviour, spoiling what might have been a ceremony of something more than ordinary poignance.

It had come about so.

There had been held previously during the evening, after the Basilica's scheduled closing hour, a service of " Departure," fastidiously private, in the presence only of the little Ostensoir-swinger " Chicklet," who, missing all the responses, had rushed about the cathedral after mice; for which the Cardinal, his sensitiveness hurt by the lad's disdain and frivolity, had afterwards confined him alone with them in the dark.

" Had it been Miguilito or Joaquin, I should not have cared a straw for their interest in the mice! But somehow this one——" the Cardinal sighed.

Adjusting in capricious abstraction his cincture, he turned towards the window.

It was a night like most.

Uranus, Venus, Saturn showed overhead their wonted lights, while in the sun-weary cloisters, brightly blue-drenched by the moon, the oleanders in all their wonder—(how swiftly fleeting is terrestrial life)—were over, and the bougainvillæas reigned instead.

" It must have been that," he murmured, smiling up at the cathedral towers.

Poor little Don Wilful. The chapter-mice, were they something so amusing to pursue? " I've a mind, do you know, to join you, boy; I declare I feel quite rompish! " he told himself, gathering up, with a jocund pounce, a heavy mantle of violet cloth-of-gold.

" Tu-whit, tu-whoo."

Two ominous owls answered one another across the troubled garden.

"I declare I feel——" his hand sought vaguely his heart: it went pit-a-pat for almost nothing now! "The strain of the diocese," he breathed, consulting a pier-glass of the period of Queen Isabella "the Ironical."

"The Court may favour Paul Orna, but in my opinion no one can rival Joey Paquin's 'line'; I should like to see him 'tailor' our Madonna; one of the worst and most expensively dressed little saints in the world," his Eminence commented, folding toga-wise the obedient tissues about his slender form.

An aspect so correctly classic evoked the golden Rome of the Imperial Cæsars rather than the so tedious Popes.

Repeating a sonorous line from Macrobius, the Cardinal measured himself a liqueur-glass of brandy.

Poor little Don Bright-eyes, alone in the obscurity. It was said a black dervish "walked" the Coro—one of the old habitués of the Mosque.

"Jewel boy. Yum-yum," he murmured, setting a mitre like a wondrous mustard-pot upon his head. *Omnia vanitas;* it was intended for Saint Peter's.

"Tu-whit, tu-whoo!"

Grasping a Bishop's stave, remotely shepherdessy, his Eminence opened softly the door.

Olé, the Styx!

Lit by Uranus, Venus and Saturn only, the con-summate tapestries on the stairs recording the Annun-ciation, Conception, Nativity, Presentation, Visitation, Purification and Ascension of the Virgin made welcome milestones.

". . . Visitation, Purification." The Primate paused on the penultimate step.

On a turn of the stair by the "Conception," a sensitive panel, chiefly white, he had the impression of a wavering shadow, as of someone following close behind.

Continuing, preoccupied, his descent, he gained a

postern door. A few deal cases, stoutly corded for departure, were heaped about it. " His Holiness, I venture to predict, will appreciate the excellence of our home-grown oranges, not to be surpassed by those of any land," the Primate purred, sailing forth into the garden.

Oh, the lovely night! Oh, the lovely night! He stood, leaning on his wand, lost in contemplation of the miracle of it.

" Kek, kek, kex."

In the old lead aqua-butt, by the Chapter-house, the gossiping bull-frogs were discussing their great horned and hoofed relations. . . .

" There was never yet one that didn't bellow! "

" Kek, kek, kex."

" *Los toros*, forsooth! "

" A blessed climate. . . ." The Primate pursued his way.

It was in the face of a little door like the door of a tomb in the cathedral's bare façade (troubled only by the fanciful shadows of the trees) that he presently slipped his key.

Olé, the Styx!

He could distinguish nothing clearly at first beyond the pale forked fugitive lightning through the triple titanic windows of the chancel.

" Sunny-locks, Don Sunny-locks? " the Cardinal cooed, advancing diffidently, as though mistrustful of meeting some charwoman's pail.

Life had prepared him for these surprises.

Traversing on his crozier a spectral aisle, he emerged upon the nave.

Flanked by the chapels of the Crucifix, of the Virgin, of the Eldest Son of God, and of divers others, it was here as bright as day.

Presumably Don April-showers was too self-abashed to answer, perhaps too much afraid. . . . " If

I recollect, the last time I preached was on the theme of Flagellation," the Primate mused, considering where it caught the moon the face of a fakir in ecstasy carved amid the corbels.

" A sermon I propose to publish," he resolved, peering into the chapel of Santa Lucia. It was prepared, it seemed, in anticipation of a wedding, for stately palms and branches of waxen peach-bloom stood all about. " Making circulation perilous," the Primate mused, arrested by the determined sound of a tenacious mouse gnawing at a taper-box.

" An admirable example in perseverance! " he mentally told himself, blinking at the flickering mauve flowers of light in the sanctuary lamps.

Philosophising, he penetrated the engrailed silver doors connecting the chapel of the Magdalen.

The chapel was but seldom without a coffin, and it was not without one now.

Since the obsequies of the brilliant Princess Eboli it had enjoyed an unbroken vogue.

Besides the triumphal monument of the beloved of Philip II, the happy (though, perhaps, not the happiest) achievement of Jacinto Bisquert, there were also mural tablets to the Duchesses of Pampeluna (*née* Mattosinhos), Polonio (*née* Charona), and Sarmento (*née* Tizzi-Azza), while the urn and ashes of the Marchioness of Orcasitas (*née* Ivy Harris) were to be found here too, far from the race and turmoil of her native New York.

" Misericordia! Are you there, boy? " the Cardinal asked, eyeing abstractedly the twin-hooded carytides that bore the fragile casket white as frozen snow containing the remains of the all-amiable princess.

Folded in dainty sleep below, he perceived the lad.

Witching as Eros, in his loose-flowing alb, it seemed profane to wake him!

68

" . . . And lead us not into temptation," the Primate murmured, stooping to gaze on him.

Age of bloom and fleeting folly: Don Apple-cheeks!

Hovering in beñison he had almost a mind to adopt the boy, enter him for Salamanca or, remoter, Oxford, and perhaps (by some bombshell codicil) even make him his heir.

"How would you like my Velasquez, boy? . . ." His Eminence's hand framed an airy caress. "Eh, child? Or my Cano Crucifix? . . . I know of more than one bottle-nosed dowager who thinks she'll get it! . . . You know my Venetian-glass, Don Endymion, is among the choicest in Spain. . . ."

There was a spell of singing silence, while the dove-grey mystic lightning waxed and waned.

Aroused as much by it as the Primate's hand, the boy started up with a scream of terror.

"Ouch, sir!"

"Olé, boy?"

The panic appeared to be mutual.

"Oufarella! . . ." With the bound of a young faun the lad was enskied amid the urns and friezes.

The heart in painful riot, the Primate dropped to a chair.

Ouching, Oléing and Oufarellaing it, would they never have done? Paternostering Phœbe Poco (shadowing her master) believed they never would. "Old ogre: why can't he be brisk about it and let a woman back to bed?" she wondered.

Thus will egotism, upon occasion, eclipse morality outright.

"And always be obedient, dear child," the Cardinal was saying; "it is one of the five things in Life that matter most."

"Which are the others, sir?"

"What others, boy?"

"Why, the other four!"

" Never mind now. Come here."

" Oh, tral-a-la, sir." Laughing like some wild spirit, the lad leapt (Don Venturesome, Don Venturesome, his Eminence trembled) from the ledge of A Virtuous Wife and Mother (Sarmento, *née* Tizzi-Azza) to the urn of Ivy, the American marchioness.

" You'd not do that if you were fond of me, boy! " The Cardinal's cheek had paled.

" But I *am* fond of you, sir! Very. Caring without caring: don't you know? "

" So you do care something, child? "

" I care a lot! . . ."

Astride the urn of Ivy—poised in air—the Chicklet pellucidly laughed.

" Tell me so again," the Cardinal begged, as some convent-bell near by commenced sounding for office before aurora.

For behind the big windows the stars were fading.

" It's to-day they draw the Lottery, sir."

" Ah; well, I had nothing in it. . . ."

" ooo5o—that's me! "

The Cardinal fetched a breath.

" Whose is it, boy? " He pointed towards the bier.

" A Poet, sir."

" A Poet? "

" The name though he had escapes me. . . ."

" No matter then."

" Where would his soul be now, sir? "

" Never mind, boy; come here."

" In the next world I should like to meet the Cid, and Christopher Columbus! "

" Break your neck, lad, and so you will."

" Pablo Pedraza too. . . ."

" Who's that, boy? "

" He was once the flower of the ring, sir; superior even to Tancos; you may recollect he was tossed and ruptured at Ronda; the press at the time was full of it."

"Our press, dear youth, our press!!!...." the Primate was about to lament, but an apologetic sneeze from a chapel somewhere in the neighbourhood of the Eldest Son of God arrested him.

It seemed almost to confirm the legend of old, Mosque-sick "Suliman," said to stalk the temple aisles.

The Cardinal twirled challengingly his stave— *Bible* v. *Koran;* a family case; cousins; Eastern, equally, each; hardy old perennials, no less equivocal and extravagant, often, than the ever-adorable *Arabian Nights!* "If only Oriental literature *sprawled* less, was more concise! It should concentrate its roses," he told himself, glancing out, inquiringly, into the nave.

Profoundly soft and effaced, it was a place full of strange suggestion. Intersecting avenues of pillared arches, upbearing waving banners, seemed to beckon towards the Infinite.

"Will you be obliged to change, sir; or shall you go straight through?"

"Straight through, boy."

"I suppose, as you cross the border, they'll want to know what you have to declare."

"I have nothing, child, but myself."

"If ooo50 is fortunate, sir, I hope to travel, too— India, Persia, Peru!!.... Ah, it's El Dorado, then."

"El Dorado, boy?" The Cardinal risked an incautious gesture.

"Oh, tral-a-la, sir." Quick as Cupid the lad eluded him on the evasive wings of a laugh; an unsparing little laugh, sharp and mocking, that aroused the Primate like the thong of a lash.

Of a long warrior line, he had always regarded disobedience (in others) as an inexcusable offence. What would have happened before the ramparts of Zaragoza, Valladolid, Leon, Burgos, had the men commanded by Ipolito Pirelli in the Peninsular War refused to obey? To be set at defiance by a youngster, a mere cock-robin, kindled elementary ancestral instincts in the Primate's veins.

" Don't provoke me, child, again."

From pillared ambush Don Prudent saw well, however, to effect a bargain.

" You'd do the handsome by me, sir; you'd not be mean? "

" Eh? . . ."

" The Fathers only give us texts; you'd be surprised, your Greatness, at the stinginess of some! "

" . . .? "

" You'd run to something better, sir; you'd give me something more substantial? "

" I'll give you my slipper, child, if you don't come here! " his Eminence warned him.

" Oufarella. . . ."

Sarabandish and semi-mythic was the dance that ensued. Leading by a dozen derisive steps Don Light-of-Limb took the nave. In the dusk of the dawn it seemed to await the quickening blush of day like a white-veiled negress.

" Olé, your Purpleship! "

Men (eternal hunters, novelty seekers, insatiable beings), men in their natural lives, pursue the concrete no less than the ideal—qualities not inseldom found combined in fairy childhood.

" Olé."

Oblivious of sliding mantle the Primate swooped.

Up and down, in and out, round and round " the Virgin," over the worn tombed paving, through Saint Joseph, beneath the cobweb banners from Barocco to purest Moorish, by early Philip, back to Turân-Shâh—" Don't exasperate me, boy "—along the raised tribunes of the choristers and the echoing coro—the great fane (after all) was nothing but a cage; God's cage; the cage of God! . . .

Through the chancel windows the day was newly breaking as the oleanders will in spring.

Dispossessed of everything but his fabulous mitre, the Primate was nude and elementary now as Adam himself.

" As you can perfectly see, I have nothing but myself to declare," he addressed some phantom image in the air.

With advancing day Don Skylark *alias* Bright-eyes *alias* Don Temptation it seemed had contrived an exit, for the cathedral was become a place of tranquillity and stillness.

" Only myself." He had dropped before a painting of old Dominic Theotocópuli, the Greek, showing the splendour of Christ's martyrdom.

Peering expectantly from the silken parted curtains of a confessional, paternostering Phœbe Poco caught her breath.

Confused not a little at the sight before her, her equilibrium was only maintained by the recollection of her status: " I'm an honest widow; so I know what men are, bless them!" And stirred to romantic memories she added: " Poor soul, he had the prettiest teeth. . . ."

Fired by fundamental curiosity, the dame, by degrees, was emboldened to advance. All over was it, with him, then? It looked as though his Eminence was far beyond Rome already.

" May God show His pity on you, Don Alvaro of my heart."

She remained a short while lost in mingled conjecture. It was certain no morning bell would wake him.

" So." She stopped to coil her brier-wood chaplet about him in order that he might be less uncovered. " It's wonderful what us bits of women do with a string of beads, but they don't go far with a gentleman."

Now that the ache of life, with its fevers, passions, doubts, its routine, vulgarity, and boredom, was over, his serene, unclouded face was a marvelment to behold. Very great distinction and sweetness was visible there, together with much nobility, and love, all magnified and commingled.

"*Adios*, Don Alvaro of my heart," she sighed, turning away towards the little garden door ajar.

Through the triple windows of the chancel the sky was clear and blue—a blue like the blue of lupins. Above him stirred the wind-blown banners in the Nave.